Bondi & Poppy

HELP HEAL THE PLANET

Written by Judith A. Proffer

Illustrated by Yoko Matsuoka

JUJU PRESS

Bondi & Poppy
Help Heal the Planet

JUJU PRESS

A division of Morling Manor Music Corporation
All rights reserved.

Illustrations by Yoko Matsuoka
Cover and interior design by designSimple

ISBN: 978-1-0880-0323-7

Printed in the United States of America

Bondi, an Australian koala,
and Poppy, a California bear,
learn the simple gestures they
can do to make a big impact.

You can make a big impact
too. A good way to learn how
to help is by volunteering
with Roots and Shoots.
rootsandshoots.org

Meet Bondi and Poppy

Each cute as a bug.

He likes
to cuddle
And she likes
to hug.

He perches
in gum trees,
sleeps much
of the day.

Across
the Pacific,
she's all about
play.

They meet up
in Hawaii, not quite
halfway.

They surf, swim,
and sport their
colorful leis.

They both
come from places
where wildfires
roam.

It's scary to worry you might lose your home.

They stare
up at the sky
way over
their heads.

Before, it was blue —
now it's yellows and reds.

Firefighters
work hard
to snuff out
the flames.

A serious
task, there's
no fun
and games.

It's time
to be mindful,
to read
and to learn.

Critters need
a safe place
to eat, sleep,
and play.

Recycle, reuse,
keep global warming
away.

AUSTRALIA

From way, way
down under,
to the California coast

CALIFORNIA

HOLLYWOOD

We must save Mama Earth — don't we need her the most?

We can all
make a difference
for this koala
and bear.

Time to
think how
to do it and
show them
we care.

Be mindful
of waste,
of not using
too much

Like water
and lights
and paper
and such.

Talk with your family
to make a smart plan.

Koalas and bears
and all living things
will love you for caring,
will give you your wings!

Our Earth
can be happy,
it's still not
too late!

Let's cuddle the planet
and say "G'day mate."

CPSIA information can be obtained
at www.ICGtesting.com
Printed in the USA
JSHW042008220123
36573JS00004B/30